SNATCHED!

THE JOURNEY BACK HOME

ESTHER GRACE

ISBN 978-1-0980-0448-4 (paperback)
ISBN 978-1-0980-0444-6 (digital)

Christian Faith Publishing, Inc.
832 Park Avenue
Meadville, PA 16335
www.christianfaithpublishing.com

Printed in the United States of America

This book is based on some of the true events of one person's life. The names of people and places have been changed to protect the innocent.

CONTENTS

ACKNOWLEDGMENTS

This book is dedicated to my Father who called me to do this and faithfully directed every step through God the Holy Spirit.

A *huge* thank you to Samaritan's Purse, who without knowing or planning this, was used by God to start the process of writing this book.

And to Titus Green, Senior Pastor of First Baptist Church Merritt Island—God used you as well to birth this book. *Thank you* also for taking the time to read it, give feedback and encourage!

For my prayer partner of almost 15 years, Elizabeth Hubert, who encouraged me through prayer and words as I stepped out— *thank you*!!

To the few dear friends that I allowed to read this book in its infancy, *thank you*! You also were such a treasured encouragement!

To my husband who patiently walked with me through all the ups and downs— you're the *best*!

For my children and grandchildren— You are *loved* and *treasured* by God and by me!

Names and Meanings

This is a list of the Hebrew names used in this book and what they mean in Hebrew or how they were spoken of in the Bible. In alphabetical order:

Abilee—the land of mourning

Avim—wicked, perverse

Avith—wicked, perverse

Chavera—friend

Daniel—God is my judge

Deborah—(as referred to in the
          Bible) prophetess,
          wife, judge (Judges 4:4)
Deron—free
Gideon—(as referred to in the
          Bible) mighty man of valor
          (Judges 6:12)
Kiba—protected
Simona—God is heard
Yigol—shall be redeemed

CHAPTER 1

SNATCHED!

Five-year-old Kiba ran with everything that was within her—crying, afraid, looking for a place to hide where Avim couldn't find her. She had never been more frightened in all her life!

Kiba's daddy, Yigol, had been taken away to prison a few years earlier when she was only two. Her momma, Simona, had divorced

Yigol and had moved in with her parents with Kiba and Deron, Kiba's older brother, in tow.

Kiba's extreme fear and sadness in losing her daddy and the home she was accustomed to eventually turned to joy as her life with her grandparents, momma, and brother had become more than she had hoped for.

Now three years later, Kiba was being chased by a man named Avim. Her momma had been dating Avim for quite a few months. Kiba knew right from the start that something was not right. Even at five years old, she had a discernment within her that there was nothing good in this man. She had avoided him at all costs, refusing to accept him into the family that she loved and enjoyed—the family where she had once again felt protected after her daddy had been taken away.

Kiba had a hard time understanding why her momma, who loved both her children with such a deep love, could fall for someone like him. She deserved so much better! *And why did she need someone else anyway? Weren't they enough?* But nevertheless, she had fallen head over heels for him.

As Kiba ran for dear life, heavy footsteps pursuing and quickly catching up with her, she darted into the dark cellar where she had spent many hours with her grandpa eating chocolate bars out of the sight of her grandma and momma—one of those lasting, joy-filled memories. Somehow, she felt she would be safe there.

She heard Avim softly calling her name. She knew this was not only a trick but was also a show for other family who might hear him. Finally she heard heavy footsteps coming down the cellar stairs. Every step seemed like a step of death to Kiba. Her heart was beating so fast she thought it would certainly burst. At the very least, she was certain he would find her because the beating of her heart was so loud in her own ears.

She could see Avim from her hiding place looking behind all the stuff that was stored in that dark basement. When he would be out of her sight, she could hear him moving things, not easily giving up. Soon she heard his footsteps so close she felt he could hear her breathing. Kiba held her breath as best as she could. After what seemed like forever, Avim peered over where she was crouched, declaring quietly so as not to be heard by others yet with a sinister tone of voice, "You can run, but I will always catch you!"

As Avim reached in to grab her, she heard the voice of her momma who, in the midst of all the commotion and unknowingly to Kiba, had made her way down the basement stairs. Her momma's voice was full of love and concern as she called out to her encouraging her not to be afraid. At that point, Avim immediately aborted his attempt. A temporary sigh of relief escaped her lips.

As her momma gently and lovingly reached into Kiba's hiding place, she held her hand and soothed her as she explained why she, Kiba, and Deron would be moving away with Avim. The temporary relief turned into panic as Kiba realized that her safe life that she had grown to love and enjoy was being snatched away from her once again. Simona helped her up and gently led her out. But Kiba's trembling hands and shaky legs were not only because of a broken heart but gave insight into the fear that coursed through every fiber of her being. A fear that would soon be realized. A fear that would be played out over the coming years of her life. Kiba, Deron, her momma, and Avim would soon be moving almost eight hundred miles away from what meant safety and security to Kiba to the sleepy little town of Abilee.

CHAPTER 2

A DARK COLD NIGHT

The trip to Abilee seemed like an eternity for Kiba. She had never even heard of this little town, but it didn't matter anyway. Her greatest fear was riding in the car with her.

In spite of her fears, sleep overtook little Kiba only to be jostled awake as the loud, old jalopy bumped and rattled down a dirt road that could hardly be called a road, all their belongings bouncing and shifting as the car hit pothole after pothole on a road that had seen very little travel. It seemed they had left any hope of civilization, except for a house with a few lights on almost a mile back.

Finally the car came to a rest at a dead-end. It was pitch dark which made everything Kiba saw seem to confirm her fears. There stood a small, dark, unpainted block building along with an outhouse that had been erected a little way from that block building now called "home". She was frozen in her seat. Deron had remained fast asleep and was being carried in by Avim. Kiba quickly jumped out and grabbed her momma's hand—the only thing she was sure of at this point in her life.

Over the days and months that followed, Kiba was always aware that something was wrong. There was a hidden dissension between her and Avim. She always knew that she had to watch her back, and Avim seemed to enjoy that. She kept this to herself as she loved her momma so much, saw her happiness, and desired with everything within her, at all costs, to protect that happiness even at her young age.

The fears that Kiba couldn't seem to shake even followed her into the outhouse. She was issued a flashlight for nighttime trips to the bathroom as her little bladder couldn't make it all night no matter how hard she tried. Avim had only sneered and told her to watch for snakes.

Kiba and Deron started school that year in that sleepy little town of Abilee. She quickly made a friend with the little girl who lived in the house with the lights on that they had passed on that dark night to her new home.

Chavera was the best of friends, and they soon became inseparable. Chavera provided Kiba with distractions that little girls should be distracted with. In addition, there was school, homework, playtime—all in the midst of what was "not right".

Simona also settled in, working hard while at the same time setting aside time for Kiba and Deron. She would come home exhausted from work but would not give in to that exhaustion until she had spent time with her children. Avim was busy working the land that surrounded that block building called "home" which gave Kiba great relief! She could sometimes forget that he was even a part of their family.

Simona, being a very young mom, had a childlikeness in her that was always seeking to play, especially with her children, many times inviting Kiba's and Deron's friends to join them. She would use her weekends to plan bonfires, treasure hunts and outdoor games making memories that would last a lifetime. And at the same time, making sure she took her children to church on Sunday—which even Avim attended from time to time.

It seemed to Kiba, at times, that just maybe—just maybe—in the midst and in spite of her deepest fears, she could once again find that safety and security that she had known and lost twice before. But it was not to be.

The ringing phone wouldn't stop. Kiba heard a tone of seriousness coming from her momma and Avim. They hurriedly ushered her and Deron to the car. Avim's dad was in a hospital over fifty miles away and was not expected to live. Kiba and Deron knew him but had not developed a relationship with him as he seemed to be very cold and indifferent. They played in the waiting room together for hours, waiting for their momma and Avim to come out of the hospital room. Finally they emerged, tired and ready to go home. It was almost dark as they all loaded in the car for the drive home.

Kiba and Deron fell asleep only to be awakened by a noise from the car and Avim cursing. Avim pulled the car onto the shoulder of the road and got out to change the flat tire. Deron, being a curious boy, went from sleepy to excited as he asked permission from his momma to get out and watch. Simona hesitantly agreed. He was ten by now and desired to learn those kinds of things. Eight-year-old Kiba, not wanting to be left out, asked her momma if she could be the one to hold the brake, which Simona had been instructed by Avim to do. Again, Simona hesitantly agreed as she assisted little Kiba with her own foot.

Suddenly, a man appeared, offering to help. He had heard the commotion and had peered out his living room window to see what it was all about. As he stood there looking on, Kiba heard him yell, "Look out! He's going to hit you!"

The explosion that took place sent Kiba into confusion. She was too short to see above the dash, but her momma's screams immediately told her something very bad had just happened.

Simona jumped out of the car on the passenger's side, and Kiba scrambled to keep up with her. As Kiba rounded the front of the car, there was Deron, lying in the middle of the road, awake and screaming in pain—bones scattered in the road beside him. Avim had been hit as well, but being a big man, had been lifted onto the hood, his hand shattering the driver's windshield. Kiba immediately felt sick not knowing what was going to happen to Deron along with concern about her momma who was crying and very obviously frightened.

When the ambulance finally arrived, the man who had come out to help wrapped his jacket around Kiba, told Simona to go with the ambulance, and whisked Kiba into his home away from all the destruction and chaos. She felt snatched again, but this time it was different. Her family left; she stayed. Her grief and fear over what had just happened swallowed up any fear of this strange man and his family who turned out to be some of the kindest people she had ever met.

Over the next weeks, Kiba remained in the care of this family, getting updates via phone calls from her momma. From time to time, she would overhear conversations that led her to believe Deron might not be coming home at all—ever. The love and concern on their faces brought a peace that she desperately needed. In the midst of their attempt to make everything as perfect as possible for her, there were times of miscommunication that caused her to even smile such as, "How do you like your eggs, Kiba?" "With the yellow runny." But what was heard was "Without the yellow." She didn't even like the whites of eggs, but for fear of hurting these nice people who were trying so hard to make things comfortable for her, she didn't say a word, eating what was served to her just as her momma had taught her.

In the midst of all of this, Avim was still being Avim. He called one day to instruct Kiba to go inside the wrecked car that was still sitting in this family's yard to find something for him. She was terrified of this car as it was a daily reminder to her of that dark, cold night, and she had steered clear of the car since then. Avim sneered at her fear and demanded that she crawl in that car and find that piece of paper. Avim was in the hospital but not badly hurt, unlike Deron. She wondered why the injuries sustained couldn't have been reversed.

After many weeks, Deron was out of the woods but would remain in the hospital for many months. Simona and Avim came to take Kiba home—or so she thought. Simona explained to her that she would need to stay at the hospital and Avim had to work the farm. Kiba would be staying with a neighbor so she could get back into school. She was distraught that momma and Deron would not be coming home too but at the same time relieved that she would not be left alone with Avim. The neighbor was nice enough but Kiba had to share a bed with her daughter who had a nightly bed-wetting issue. Kiba would snuggle tightly with the edge of the bed, but many nights that didn't suffice.

Over the months that followed, she greatly missed her momma and Deron and couldn't wait to be a family again. In the meantime, she was staying even closer to Chavera's house which gave her—among school, homework and play—a much needed outlet. And even though Avim was not far away, there were very few occasions that she had to see or even talk to him.

CHAPTER 3

A FAMILY SEPARATED

Kiba was so excited! Her momma and Deron were coming home—finally! After many months in the hospital, with Simona going back-and-forth spending most of her time at Deron's side, he was being released to come home. Kiba couldn't contain her excitement even though it meant back to the farm with

Avim. She had spent many nights in her shared, temporary bed quietly crying, just wanting things to be normal again.

But normal was not to return soon. After the homecoming, the celebration, and the excitement followed a new adjustment for everyone. Simona found herself trying to adapt to being Deron's nurse as he was still in casts after multiple surgeries. At the same time, Simona was trying to make up to Kiba for the time she had been gone, trying to get back to work and all the other things that still needed to be done. Deron was trying to adjust being at home, still in pain and not having the "real-nurse" care that he got in the hospital. And Kiba—Kiba was torn between being so excited about them being home while still always looking for ways to be away from Avim. Avim was still being Avim.

Deron could not walk yet. He was still in a wheelchair and needed a lot of assistance.

Kiba was not aware of his diagnosis—that he would have to go somewhere to learn to walk again. As Simona shared this with Kiba, her heart sank. *Not again! Family separated—again? Where would he go? How far away? How often would we get to see him? Will he be okay?*

Simona tried to assure Kiba in all of her answers to these questions. She tried to explain that while Deron would be going far away from them, it would only be for about a year, and he would be at a place close to their grandparents. Kiba felt a lot of different emotions. She was happy for Deron that he would be reunited with their grandparents, and at the same time sad that they would be separated again. *And just why couldn't all three of us go? Why couldn't it be like it was before?* Kiba ran to her room crying. *Why? Why does it have to be this way?*

In the proceeding weeks, Kiba tried to imagine what her life would look like without

Deron. While the two of them often fought, she loved him; and yet another separation of family was overwhelming to little Kiba.

All too soon, the day came to pack up Deron for his new, temporary home at a crippled children's hospital. The three of them—Simona, Deron, and Kiba—piled in the car for the long trip. Kiba felt different emotions all at the same time—excitement that she would get to see her grandparents yet sad that she and her momma would have to return to Abilee—and without Deron.

Over the next year, Kiba settled into life. She missed Deron terribly, but Simona once again had done everything within her power as a loving momma to try to make things as normal as possible. Every chance Simona and Kiba got they would travel to see Deron and her grandparents. But these were few and far between as money and time wouldn't allow such a long trip. However, the few occasions gave Kiba a respite from Avim.

And once again Chavera was a welcomed distraction, a friend by her side helping her in the midst of her loneliness without Deron. She kept Kiba busy after school and on the weekends while school and homework filled the rest of the day.

Finally the day came when Simona and Kiba loaded up for the long trip to bring Deron home and another chance to reunite with her grandparents. Deron could walk now, and Kiba couldn't wait to get back to normal.

Deron seemed to be different when he came home. Simona comforted Kiba by explaining that he too had been through many changes—not just mentally and socially but also physically. But he seemed to adjust after some time, and the two of them were back to spending their weekends and summers outside, digging in the dirt for Indian artifacts which Deron loved to collect. Kiba loved to find them too but didn't care to collect them and would gleefully present her finds to Deron. It was good to have him home.

By this time, Kiba was experiencing the hormonal changes that happen to young, preteen girls. She was beginning to develop in areas that at times were exciting and in other ways seemed just downright unfair. *Would things ever stop changing?*

But she wasn't the only one that noticed her changing body.

Chapter 4

Evil Lurks

Kiba had busied herself with all the normal things of life that she could possibly dream of that was normal. But that "not right" feeling was coming upon her once again with an overwhelming dread. As she grew and matured, Avim changed. While his sneers still came from time to time, most of his attention seemed to be diverted to her ever-changing body. She grew to hate Avim, feeling his eyes on her every time the two of them were in the same place. She would catch him looking at her and shoot him the most hateful glances she could muster, which would only cause sneers in return. Many times she would run to her room and immediately lock the door behind her.

She would find herself worrying about Avim peering in the crack between the door and the wall while she was in the bathroom, always pulling the shower curtain shut while she took a bath. It seemed evil was lurking everywhere he was.

Kiba felt unprotected, and she dreamed often of what it would have been like if her daddy had not gone to prison. He, most certainly, would have protected her. She would jump on her bicycle almost every evening after school and ride for hours up and down that lonely stretch of dark road that separated her from Chavera's house dreaming of what life could have been like. She would even wonder if her daddy was out of prison yet as there had been no contact almost from the beginning. *And if she needed somewhere to go, would he want her? But how would she ever leave her momma and Deron?*

She knew she never could! She felt as if her only protection was her own vises, and she seemed to need them more and more every day. Her momma would have most certainly been her protector had she known. But Kiba couldn't prove unwanted stares, and if she could, she wouldn't anyway. Once again, she felt the need to protect her momma's happiness. Kiba felt she was born with a protective spirit that would much rather take a hit herself than to bring any trouble to someone she loved.

And Kiba had Chavera to confide in. Young Chavera listened, advised, and commiserated with her as only two teenage girls could. Chavera would often get angry about what was taking place and just couldn't understand why Kiba wouldn't go straight to her momma. But as their friendship grew and Chavera accompanied her and Simona in all kinds of activities, there were two things that Chavera did come to understand: that Kiba and Simona had a very special momma-and-daughter relationship, and that Kiba would protect her momma at all costs.

Chavera herself grew to love Simona. Simona loved life, loved to laugh, loved to play but could also get serious when the occasion called for seriousness. She worked hard at providing what she felt her children needed, and graciously included their friends.

At the same time, Chavera was very aware of some scary rumors going around the little town of Abilee concerning Avim. As rumors typically go, everyone heard them except family. But Chavera was constantly keeping Kiba updated as there were many sleepovers where the two of them would lie awake for hours and talk—not just about the rumors but teenage girl stuff as well. Kiba had no doubt in her mind that the rumors Chavera shared were true. After all, she lived in the same house with Avim. She got to know more about him than she cared to know.

As time went on, this seemed to be Kiba's "normal". She seemed to be becoming a pro at adapting to change, figuring out her options at each turn, and exercising those options when needed. At this point in her life, her motto became *Sink or swim; you are on your own,* even though several years earlier she had met Friend who had promised He would never leave her side and would always help her. With all the commotion, emotions, trouble, and just life in general, Kiba wasn't certain He meant it and had soon forgotten Him and what He had said.

Kiba found herself desperate for what she thought was love from a man. She was popular at school, especially among the guys. She got many compliments about her beauty—but believed none of them. She was a strawberry-blonde—at the time, mostly strawberry—who despised her hair color, didn't appreciate being called "Red" as a nickname, and would often look at herself in the mirror and declare loudly that she must be the ugliest human being on the face of the earth.

Nevertheless, she attracted a lot of attention from a lot of guys and snatched it all up, reveling in it—until they made the mistake of telling her they loved her. Something would happen in Kiba that she herself couldn't even explain. *Wasn't that what she longed to hear?* All she knew was that it seemed that was her only goal—and once she heard it, it was time to move on and hear it from yet another guy.

Not only did she date with an attitude of "no rules, no strings attached," but at the same time, she became a leader among her peers—heading up all kinds of wild parties and coming up with mischievous things to do in that small little town of Abilee that would cause most to blush, such as hopping the fence around the country club pool and daring everyone to go skinny dipping—always planning for a good time.

Kiba was busy doing life, protecting herself, and immersing herself and others in all the fun—right or wrong—that she could possibly dream up. She was unprepared for what was next.

CHAPTER 5

HOOKED UP

Kiba awoke to a bright, sunny day. Everything that had become normal to her seemed normal that day. But Simona had become increasingly sick over the past couple of months, going in for doctor visits often. One night, she sat Kiba down to explain to her that her kidneys were failing due to the measles that had settled in her kidneys as a teenager and had continued to do damage all these years. Momma would have to go on dialysis, hoping at some point for a kidney transplant. Without this, she would surely die. There were no dialysis options in the little town of Abilee, so she would have to travel to a city that was three hours away to get the help she needed. And she would have to do this three times a week.

Kiba was reeling with all kinds of thoughts. She could not even begin to think about momma dying, so she moved on to thinking about what it might look like to have momma gone from home three days a week, leaving just her and Deron—and of course, Avim. She had many questions for Simona who gently explained what the plan would be.

In all of the fears that Kiba was experiencing, her momma shared that this time Kiba's grandparents would be coming to live with them to help in any way they could. Once again, her emotions were mixed—so excited to have her grandparents be a part of their daily lives again yet fearful of what might happen to her momma.

The next several months were a whirl-wind. Kiba's grandparents moved into the block building called home that Avim and his dad had expanded over the years. It now included an indoor bathroom and several bedrooms. When Simona's kidneys completely failed, she started dialysis right away with her parents transporting her back-and-forth to the big city three times a week. Kiba and Deron went to school and spent summers doing kid things while Avim worked the land—and harassed Kiba every chance he could.

Kiba continued to fight the fight that she had convinced herself was only hers to fight, protecting herself at all costs while also feeling as if she needed to protect her now sick momma. There were rumors that Avim was consoling himself with other women, and Kiba believed them all. She hated him even more for what he was doing to her momma.

Kiba would come home from school every day and do her best to pitch in so that her momma wouldn't be burdened with things such as cooking, housework, etc. Her grandparents helped but were mostly busy taking care of Simona. But just having them there almost made it seem like normal again with the exception of Avim and now her sickly momma.

Then came the day that it was announced that Simona would be taking her dialysis treatments from home. Kiba's heart skipped a beat as she was once again comforted that all her family would be home every day together. The plan was that Avim would add on to the block home a room set up for a dialysis machine and a hospital bed. Kiba's grandma would be trained on the machine and would become Simona's nurse.

Three days a week, Simona was hooked up to dialysis all the while continuing to encourage Kiba and Deron from her hospital bed even when she was not having a good day. It was hard for Kiba to watch her beloved momma so sick. She missed their times together—the fun, the laughter, and the daily life things that her momma made so special. On her momma's good days, once again, Simona would try to make up for the days that weren't so good.

In the meantime, while Kiba thought things might be returning to somewhat normal even if it was a "new normal", she overheard conversation that dialysis was not working as it should for her momma. Her body was wearing down, so the doctors immediately moved her up on the transplant list, which had become her only hope.

Lots of prayer went up for Simona. Kiba begged God for a new kidney for her momma. She just wanted her back, the momma she had always known. Kiba had taken a job at a local diner as a way to earn a little money which also proved to be a great distraction. Now life was busier than ever, and she was able to distance herself from Avim even more. And the wait was on for her momma's new kidney.

The day came! The phone rang loudly at the diner where Kiba worked. The manager who answered immediately shot a concerned yet excited look at Kiba and told her it was an emergency. She ran to the phone to hear Simona telling her they were leaving right away for the big city. A kidney had been found, and there was no time to waste. Kiba was excited and nervous all at the same time.

Was she getting her momma back? What if something went wrong? How long would she be gone from home? Not only would she be gone, but her grandparents would be gone too, leaving Deron and Kiba alone with Avim.

Kiba found herself once again applying her motto, *Sink or swim; you are on your own.* Her grandparents kept in touch letting them know how the surgery was going and the recovery afterward. When her momma was stronger Avim, Deron, and Kiba went to be with her. Kiba was overjoyed at her momma's new strength even though still in the recovery mode. She looked radiant, was smiling, and everyone was celebrating and hopeful. Simona returned home after several months in the hospital. She was quickly getting back to her fun self, laughing and enjoying life.

Kiba, in the meantime, had been overwhelmed by the kindness of her teachers. She had never even considered that others knew or even cared about what was going on in their family, but as she returned to school after having missed many days, she found that not only had she been excused from mid-term exams but was given good grades for the exams she didn't even take. Her home economics teacher even made a dress for her that counted toward her final grade and gave her a good grade for it as well. Ahhh! The reality of goodness and kindness even in the midst of such turmoil. It would be the little big things like that that would eventually become a part of Kiba's story—unbeknownst to her.

CHAPTER 6

REVELATION OF DEATH

It had been a three-year-long journey. Kiba's grandparents packed up to return to their home, and even though she was sad to see them leave, it was softened by her momma being momma again. Simona was not only home, but she picked up right where she left off before she became so sick. Once again, even though Kiba and Deron were teenagers now, hanging out with their friends every chance they got, Simona was a big part of their lives in various though individual ways.

For instance, there was pizza and comic book night every Wednesday. Simona would stop to buy groceries on her way home from work, picking up pizza and comic books, which they would excitedly anticipate even at their age. It was a tradition. Then there were Friday night bonfires—roasting hotdogs and marshmallows and eating potato chips and the white-powdered sugar-coated donuts until they were sick—most always in the company of several of their friends that lived in the area, all at Simona's organization.

Simona and Kiba continued to have a very special momma-and-daughter kind of relationship, sometimes looking more like they were best friends, which they were in a sense. There were even those in that small town, not knowing them, who thought they were sisters. When Kiba and her friends would decide to go into the next town which was much larger for dinner and a movie or just some shopping, her friends, particularly Chavera, would often suggest that Simona be invited.

Kiba was always grateful that her friends felt that way. She loved inviting her momma along on their not-so-mischievous outings even knowing they would have to behave if her momma was there. But there was guaranteed fun and laughter.

Chavera would remind Kiba from time to time of how Kiba and Simona's relationship was much different than most mommas and daughters. They would spend hours at the piano, laughing and singing together. Simona would play while they would both sing. When Deron would come in to ask what they were doing, they would teasingly assure him that they were practicing to perform at church that next Sunday. He would plead with them not to while they would pretend to not understand why he felt that way and would keep right on practicing.

And the laughter—there was lots of it. A laughter and a voice that Simona and Kiba shared that not even family could tell apart if they were not in the same room with them. Then there were the card games. Simona and Kiba both loved playing cards and were very competitive, starting tournaments between themselves, playing most every night and keeping a score card of wins. There would be a set end date to determine who the champion was.

It was after one of these card games that Simona requested Kiba's undivided attention. Her momma could get serious at times, but Kiba didn't like the seriousness. She tried to bring back the game mood, but momma was determined to have Kiba *really* hear what she was getting ready to say. So she reluctantly settled down and gave Simona her full attention.

But what Simona shared with Kiba sent her into a panic—and then denial. Simona was a godly momma who loved Jesus. She had made many mistakes in her life but had been redeemed and personally knew her Savior. In one of her many talks with Father, He revealed to her that she would not live to be very old. He did not give her a time frame, only a time reference. Simona shared how she had pleaded with Father not to let her suffer as she had with the kidney issue. And then she shared with Kiba what she had asked of Father—to die instantly in a car accident.

Kiba was shaken to the core. First, this just was not going to happen and she wasn't going to acknowledge it. Secondly, she was horrified and couldn't understand why her momma would ask to die in such a tragic way. Simona calmly and quietly explained her reasoning using words such as "instant", "no suffering", and "not knowing what hit me". After some very serious time of talk, Kiba got up and went to her room. She wrote off the conversation, denying the likelihood that any such thing would or could ever happen to her precious momma. It just was not going to be!

Life and time moved on for the next couple of years. In that period of time, Deron was in a head-on collision which caused a sickening fear followed by a quick relief as he was okay in spite of a totaled car. It seemed to Kiba like there was a time limit to peace.

Kiba was continuing to blossom and mature, now being close to graduating from high school. She had spent a lot of time the past thirteen years or so of her life dodging Avim's looks and remarks, locking doors behind her and staying away from home as much as possible. Then came that pivotal day—a day that changed everything. A day that started a firestorm of a different nature for Kiba.

Kiba had not seen it coming nor had she planned this kind of reaction. But as she was walking down the hall of what had now been home for years, Avim was hot on her heels, threatening her in every way possible. Something inside her snapped, and she spun around, eyes locked on Avim's eyes, and dared him to *ever* lay a hand on her in any way. The time that followed seemed long, and fear screamed loud in her ears.

Avim was a big man and Kiba was small in stature. Avim had been taught by his cold, domineering dad that women and children were only to be seen and not heard. And she happened to be both. Coupled with what she knew about Avim's wicked heart, she was certain he was going to kill her.

The clock in the hallway ticked louder than ever. Kiba could hear her own heart beat in her ears and knew she should probably run. But something kept her feet firmly planted. They were in the house alone with no one to hear or see. Suddenly, Avim wheeled around and stormed off, but not before Kiba saw a hatred in his eyes that far exceeded all the sneering and lustful looking that he had ever done.

Kiba knew there was trouble ahead.

CHAPTER 7

HEAD-ON

As Avim's hatred for Kiba continued to kindle, he shot looks and comments at her of a different kind, and she shot back at him with hatred of her own. She had just graduated from high school, and Deron had married and moved on. Kiba had moved to an apartment to get away from Avim, but not only did she miss her momma, she had trouble surviving working only minimum-wage jobs. She still had planned "dates" with her momma, but it just wasn't the same.

Every Monday, Simona would cook Kiba's favorite meal which would end in another card game with the two of them. Every Wednesday was a lunch date with her momma, which of course, Simona paid for.

This went on for about six months with Kiba and Simona talking and planning for Kiba to move back. She was torn between missing her momma, being broke, and the thoughts of living in the same house with Avim again. Her momma knew she missed her and knew she was struggling financially but knew nothing of Kiba's struggle with Avim. Kiba had found a roommate which had helped financially, but the roommate was getting married and soon to move. She knew she could not afford to stay in her apartment on her own, though she had enjoyed not looking over her shoulder and locking doors behind her.

Monday came, dinner and cards. Wednesday came, lunch date with her momma. Then Thursday came. Kiba was still asleep as she worked a nine-to-five job down-town Abilee. She was abruptly awakened by her roommate knocking loudly on her door. The door opened before Kiba could say a word. There stood her roommate, looking as if she had seen a ghost.

Kiba was informed that her boss and his wife were downstairs waiting for her. She had gone to work for a local attorney who special-ized in divorce and was training her to draw up and file with the court any needed papers to lighten his load. She had gotten to expe-rience more than she wanted to see, always amazed at what went on behind the scenes in that little town—things that were far from legitimate and even farther from any standard of morals. But she had become accustomed to life not being what she would call "fair" or "right" and just went with the flow, finding herself mixing in and even becoming comfortable with things that she knew were not right.

As Kiba piled out of bed wrapping her robe around her, she grumbled all the way down the townhouse stairs. *Are you kidding me? Just whose divorce is so important that it can't wait 'til the office opens at nine?* She made it to the platform where she would turn to descend the last few stairs. But that didn't happen. Her boss and his wife were standing at the foot of those stairs to meet her. He told her to go get dressed because her momma had been in a terrible accident. As he was talking, his wife just turned and walked away into the living room and sat down.

Kiba didn't say a word. There was no time. She raced back up the stairs, not even feeling her feet touch them. All she knew was her momma needed her. She also knew that because of her momma's kidney transplant, there were certain things she couldn't have—certain medicines they couldn't give her. *Would they even be aware of her transplant?* She had to get there fast. She had to let her know that she was there and would do everything she could to protect her from losing her kidney. She threw on the first set of clothes she found, grabbed her purse and her keys, and went racing back down the stairs.

Her boss told her to put her keys away; he was driving. She didn't argue because that would have cost precious time. She thought it strange that his wife didn't follow them out the door but didn't take time to worry about that either. She jumped in the passenger's side of the car and instructed him that she needed to go to the big city where the transplant had taken place as she was certain that was where they would take her. It didn't occur to Kiba at that time that what she was thinking earlier didn't even make sense with what she was thinking now.

It didn't matter. Her boss, who had had a couple of stiff drinks before coming over, knowing their close relationship and that he was getting ready to destroy her world, slammed his fist into the steering wheel as he loudly and quickly shouted out, "Now Kiba, your momma didn't make it!"

Kiba heard someone screaming and knew it was her but couldn't feel the scream coming from her throat. First she saw lots of black with flashes of light. Then her vision came back and she saw people getting in their cars, leaving for work or school, waving and throwing kisses to their families. *How could they? How can they act as if everything is right in this world when there will never be anything right in my world again?*

Her boss drove her to the local emergency room. By this time, Kiba had already decided that if she got there in time, she could convince her momma not to die. As soon as the car pulled into the back entrance to the emergency room, even before it stopped, she jumped out of the car and hit the ground running. She ran into the emergency room and demanded to see her momma. She was gently but firmly told that was not possible. There were people lined up in the emergency room who had been called ahead of time for support. Kiba will never forget the looks on their faces. She lost it—demanding, pleading, threatening—anything to gain access to her momma, still being convinced that she could beg her not to die. She knew her momma would listen. She wouldn't leave her! She just knew.

The funeral that followed was a blur. There was her young momma—only thirty-eight years old—once so full of life and laughter now still, quiet, with lots of funeral makeup on. *How could this be?* Kiba had picked out the dress she was in because it was her momma's favorite. She also had them put a necklace with a heart charm on it around her neck. Kiba had given that to her for Mother's Day one year and wanted her to keep it even as others suggested she might want to keep that for herself. "No, momma's taking my heart with her."

She tried to reach in and hug her momma one last time but was quickly intercepted by watchful funeral directors. They tried to gently explain that her momma was hurt badly and that hugging her, holding her hand, or even touching her was not an option. She was horrified in the midst of such unimaginable grief. A well-meaning friend even tried to comfort her by telling her that her momma "didn't even know what hit her"—words that

Kiba would recall much later that her own momma had shared with her concerning her request to Father of how she wanted to die and why.

She spent the next weeks, and even months, in a pit of deep grief—a pit that there seemed no way out of. She wasn't worried about what she would do or where she would go. All she could think about was her momma, trying to wrap her mind around her being gone, reliving what little she knew about the accident, asking herself a lot of "what ifs," and playing totally different scenarios in her head than the one that actually played out.

But Chavera, who also was grieving Simona's loss, was concerned about losing Kiba too in more ways than one. All the laughter, all the fun times, and even the mischievous times had come to an abrupt halt. Not just temporarily, but for many months.

And would Kiba have to leave? Where would she go? Chavera had some questions for her, but she had no answers. She was too busy trying to figure out things that couldn't be figured out or that didn't matter, such as: *What were her momma's last thoughts? Did she need her and realize she wasn't there? Did she experience pain? Did she even see the other car coming?*

She had been hit head-on by another car at a high rate of speed. The driver and passenger had just been released from jail for DUI and were late for work. They passed a car in front of them at an estimated speed of over a hundred miles per hour and collided with her momma.

Kiba's life from that point on for many months consisted of work and only doing what had to be done, such as cleaning out her momma's workstation where she had worked so hard and made so many friends. As she entered that building, people stopped what they were doing, turned off their noisy machines, and stood quietly in honor of her momma as she walked by. And Kiba was tearfully and gratefully reminded of who her momma had been as a young man, who struggled mentally and emotionally, approached her with his head hanging telling her how much he had loved her momma. She had reached out to him and his young wife who was also mentally challenged by giving them a wedding shower. Kiba had recalled the story Simona had shared with her. It seemed all kinds of showers were readily given for others, but theirs had been "passed over". Simona was mortified. While she didn't feel throwing showers was her gift, she put one together for this beautiful couple—an act of kindness that had not been forgotten.

Then there was the phone call. Kiba had almost come to dread the ring of a phone or a knock on the door. The man on the other

end—kind, compassionate, apologetic—
carefully and gently told Kiba her momma's
car was getting ready to be towed away, but
her purse and other personal items were still
in it. A detail that had never even entered
Kiba's thoughts. He had called Avim several
times over the months after the accident, giving him the chance to claim her things, but
he had never responded. This kind man knew
Kiba wouldn't want her momma's things to
be lost and explained it was against the law
for him to touch her personal things.

It was the first time Kiba had even seen
her momma's wrecked car. She pried open the
driver's side door and stood horrified by the
scene. There was lots of glass, dried blood, and
other unidentifiable matter. She sat down in
the seat and robotically started gathering her
precious momma's things while at the same
time trying to imagine what her momma
must have went through, getting physically

sick and choking back desperate tears. There was her purse, opened and spilled out. Her now rotten lunch scattered all over the car. Those things. That event. Those things that are forever etched in the mind and heart.

Kiba visited her momma's grave often to talk. She knew her momma wasn't really there, but that was the last place she saw her as they lowered her into the ground.

As she had lots of time to reflect in the coming months going through every emotion imaginable, sometimes many times a day, Friend, whom she had met years ago but had not been in close contact with, suddenly showed up by her side as He had promised. "I see you are hurting, Kiba." She didn't understand why His voice was so comforting and reassuring. All she knew was she needed that. She needed Friend. She told Him all about her momma which He seemed to already know. She told Friend how ashamed she was of her wild lifestyle even after meeting Him personally at church many years ago. He also seemed to know about that. She told Friend a lot of things, pouring out her broken heart that she was certain would never mend. He didn't condemn her but lovingly listened, comforted, and encouraged Kiba right where she was.

She continued to talk to Friend a lot. It seemed He was always there when she needed Him. *How on earth was that possible? Why did He care so much?* She had never felt such love! *Was this what she had been looking for in all of her dating relationships?* No, it seemed to be so much more.

CHAPTER 8

EVIL TIMES TWO

Kiba listened to Friend and was comforted and encouraged. She had moved back into her momma's house with Avim shortly after the funeral. She knew that was not a wise choice but seemed to have run out of options. Deron was married and soon to be a daddy and would have gladly taken her in, but she knew things weren't going well in their marriage and didn't want to do anything to harm it more. Kiba's grandparents begged her to come, but she didn't want to leave her friends, and yes, even her momma's grave. Besides, Avim had seemed to be brought low by losing momma as her laughter and joy were contagious even for him. And Kiba knew she needed time to save money so she could find a place of her own.

Things went fairly well—for a little while. Kiba even surprisingly had compassion for Avim as he was hurting too. But her compassion seemed to be mistaken by him for something entirely different. Kiba rejected his advance, and his hatred seemed to return in an instant. She needed a place to stay; so once again, she found herself staying very busy working several jobs, saving money, and not being home when he was there. And it seemed Avim needed her to be there as he had given up farming the land and had a job that many times called him out-of-town. It was working—for now.

In the meantime, Chavera was passing on information to Kiba about fierce rumors that were being spread about her by Avim. It seemed to be his way of showing his hatred, almost in a cowardly manner. She would get angry from time to time, along with Chavera, but words were the least of her worries. She had been tipped off through Chavera who had been informed by someone else who was "in the know", that Avim was a very danger-ous person with involvement with the Ku Klux Klan. The KKK, as they were known, were wicked and had a reputation for even being murderers. Kiba believed every word and started working harder to get enough money to leave.

As Avim's hatred grew even more, Kiba, who was desperately working three jobs, started receiving threatening phone calls. The calls would always start around 6:30 p.m. and be intermittent all night, ending around 7:00 a.m. The man would threaten her with all kinds of unimaginable things including death. She was terrified and called the police several times. Every time she called, the small town police department of Abilee would assure her that it was just one of her ex-boyfriends and she would be fine. She knew better as most of the guys she dated were much nicer than she deserved and would have come to her defense had she asked them. The police would also suggest at times that maybe she was too emotional after losing her momma and that it wasn't as bad as it seemed.

But Chavera had news for Kiba. News that came from her "good source" who was too afraid of the KKK but wanted to see to it that Kiba knew what she was up against. It seemed that popular opinion was that there were two groups on the police force—those who were a part of the KKK and those who were too afraid to go against them. Kiba realized she would not be able to count on them for help.

She had forgotten about Friend—again. She was back to *Sink or swim; you're on your own*. So she devised a plan. Chavera was with her when the phone calls started again that next night and kept remarking how convenient it was that Avim was out-of-town. Much to Chavera's surprise and horror, Kiba invited her caller to come over. She had had enough. The phone calls had gone on for weeks, and she needed her sleep. Chavera pleaded with Kiba to go home with her; and when she couldn't convince her, apologized with tears for leaving her. Kiba understood. She loved Chavera and didn't want her to get hurt or to be any more caught up in this than she already was. But Kiba, as terrified as she was, knew she couldn't walk away from this.

Otherwise, she would truly have to run—but where?

Kiba stayed—and really wasn't sure why. She didn't feel courageous. It was more like desperation mixed with grief. Kiba loaded her .38 revolver, turned all the lights on in the house, positioned herself in a spot where she felt she would be hidden but could still see the front door—and waited.

Chavera had warned Kiba that whoever this caller was would surely kill her. Kiba agreed but with somewhat a different spin. Kiba's desperate thought was that someone would most certainly die that night—be it her or him. If it was him, she felt he would get his just reward. If it was her, she would be with momma. It was a win-win for her. But even with such an outlook, it just was not in her heart to kill someone. She never dreamed she would ever find herself in this kind of situation, not in her wildest dreams.

However, *sink or swim, Kiba*. She had learned in her short life that sometimes you just have to face things head-on—and alone.

Kiba waited for what seemed an eternity. She thought that surely her heart would give out as it was beating so fast. The sound of her heartbeat rang in her ears loudly again as she was recalling the incident in the hallway with Avim. Finally she heard a very loud car coming down that lonely, dark stretch of road. It sounded like it was on its last leg. While the noise seemed ominous, at the same time it was trackable. She could almost tell the exact spot that he was at any given time.

Kiba cocked her .38 revolver. She waited. The loud car came to a stop and idled. She listened for a door to open and close but was not able to pick up on any such sound. She found herself holding her breath, afraid that even her breathing would give her away. After what seemed like an eternity, there was a sudden acceleration as the car sped off into the distance. *What had just happened?* Kiba waited for a while longer wondering if someone had been dropped off and the whole "car leaving suddenly" was just a ploy.

Another eternity passed. Finally Kiba unfolded from her hiding place quietly and carefully. She was still quite terrified—and now she had a cocked .38 to try to release without firing. She slowly and successfully released the hammer, ran to her room with all the lights still on, locked her door, put the .38 on her nightstand, and tried to get some sleep. But sleep would not come. She was still on guard, hearing every noise and wondering if it was him, heart still thumping loudly. And at the same time, her thoughts were racing. There was something strangely familiar about the sound of that car.

Exhaustion finally caused Kiba to go to sleep in spite of her guarded fear. The phone startled her from a sound sleep. She jumped out of bed not sure what the noise was but was immediately returned to her awareness of fear. Then the phone rang again. Kiba answered. It was him. Something snapped in Kiba again—as it had with Avim. All the exhaustion and terror turned to anger. It was Kiba's turn. She berated him for leaving, calling him a coward. He hung up. The rest of the night was quiet.

The next morning, after Kiba had had at least a couple of hours of sleep, she began to think about the familiar sound of the car. She knew it but couldn't place it. But now she felt empowered and encouraged to sit down and take inventory of what she knew. First the sound of the car. Then she focused on the timing of the phone calls. They always started at a certain time in the evening and ended at a certain time in the morning. She had assumed previously that this man had a job, and those hours were just his convenient hours to harass and threaten.

Then a light bulb came on. The car! Avim had a twin whose name was Avith. They were of kindred spirit as well. Kiba had always avoided Avith, which was easy, as he was busy harassing his own family with the same kindred spirit that Avim had. Avim and Avith carpooled to their job together, which is why she was so familiar with the sound of that old car. Then Kiba turned to the timing of the phone calls. It wasn't so much because he worked, but rather because his wife worked—a nurse—night shift—7:00 p.m. to 7:00 a.m.

Kiba knew Avith's daughter who had attended the same school with her and was in some of the same classes together. She had shown up many times at school with bruises. When she wasn't at school, it was because she had run away. The police always found her and brought her back home. She had tried to tell them what Avith was doing to her, but she either wasn't believed or had the same issue with the small town police force that Kiba had. She was an extremely unhappy and angry young woman. Kiba had locked eyes with her one day at school after she had just been returned from one of her runaway events. She saw something very telling in her eyes and knew she was telling the truth.

Avith! While Kiba was still very afraid knowing how he treated his own family, she felt some relief as now she knew who her harasser all this time had been. And she had a plan! She gathered up all the courage she could muster having learned that men like that truly are cowards. She had revealed his character rightly on that last phone call. But now she had something more than a name of his character to call him—his real name. She was still aware of his wicked heart and knew she needed to be careful but at the same time knew in her heart that what she was getting ready to do should that phone ring again that night was the right thing to do.

Suddenly, the phone rang and jostled Kiba from her thoughts. It was Chavera. The relief in her voice when Kiba answered soon turned into tears. Chavera hadn't slept all night either, wondering with great fear what was happening to Kiba. Kiba recounted the night quickly as she couldn't wait to reveal what she had figured out. Chavera wasn't surprised about Avith and quickly agreed that everything sure added up. But like Kiba, Chavera was concerned about what that might mean, especially if he knows he's been found out. She told Chavera her plan, and by now, Chavera knew that Kiba would most certainly have to carry it out. It seemed to be her best shot, short of running.

Kiba made her way through the day, exhausted yet with an exhilarating determination that gave her momentum she didn't think was possible after having lost so much sleep, not just the night before but the several preceding weeks of constant middle-of-the-night phone calls. She had thought about taking the phone off the hook so she could get some sleep, but then she wouldn't know where he was and still would not be able to sleep. The phone calls kept her assured he was on the other end of the line and not outside her door. But now, she felt as if she at least had a weapon in her hand that she could use. She now knew something she hadn't known before—something of great importance—and as the saying goes, "Knowing is half the battle."

Kiba waited for the phone to ring that night. She didn't have to wait long. Almost on queue at 6:30 p.m., the phone rang. She had every emotion imaginable coursing through her body. She answered. It was him. He started threatening but barely got out any words before she started in on him. "I know who you are, Avith! Coward!"

She had planned to say a lot more as her anger had a lot to unleash on him and it seemed to take over any fear in her at that point. But Avith hung up—immediately! It seemed that the tables had turned, at least for now. She found some comfort in that and was even more convinced than ever that "coward" most certainly was the right characterization for men like him.

The phone was quiet the rest of the night. And the night after. And the following nights. Avim came home from his trip. Chavera was convinced that he had instigated the whole thing, but Kiba wasn't sure. Avith didn't really need Avim to instigate anything. They both seemed to follow their own wicked thoughts without any help from anyone else.

CHAPTER 9

MOVING ON

By this time, Kiba had saved enough money to move. She didn't have a lot but wasn't afraid to work and knew she could make it. Chavera's family invited her to move in with them to save a little while longer which she was grateful for. In the meantime, she continued working her three jobs saving every penny she could. She had a very strict budget and would even go without food to stay on that budget.

Kiba desperately searched for a place that she could afford. There just wasn't anything in that small town that would fit into her budget. Then the phone rang. It was Avim. He had bought a broken down old trailer park and needed someone to run it. She wasn't sure what he was up to as there seemed to be nothing good in him, but she was desperate; and the deal fit her budget. She could live in one of the trailers as long as she managed all the others, mowed the half acre and took care of anything that needed to be taken care of. Kiba was already working so much she wasn't sure how she could do that. But once again, Chavera stepped up to the plate. "I want to go with you and help you." What a friend! Those words from a good friend sounded vaguely familiar, reminding Kiba of Friend whom she hadn't talked to in some time.

Kiba and Chavera moved into the only trailer available. The front door didn't close all the way. There were holes in the floor, and wind came in around the windows enough to blow the curtains—with the windows shut. But it was a roof over their heads. Kiba and Chavera stuffed rags in the holes in the floor to keep out rodents, roaches, and other unwelcomed guests, tried to bend the door so it would shut better, and taped plastic around the windows. Kiba settled in to what she knew could only be her temporary home— once again. She worked, she saved, and she worked some more. Not much time for a social life even though she managed to make time for a little fun every so often. Dating had pretty much ended for the most part with a boyfriend here and there. Kiba had a plan: to continue to save until she could move, but this time far from Abilee.

Life, however different from what Kiba had planned, was moving on again just as Friend had counseled her to do in His words of encouragement. All the while, she was going to church as Simona had taught her to do, but that was all the time she found to give to Friend.

Just as everything seemed to be as normal as it could be considering the circumstances, a loud sounding car pulled into Kiba's driveway. She immediately recognized that sound. Chavera looked out the window and yelled what Kiba already knew, "It's him! It's Avith!"

In broad daylight, there stood Avith. He had even had the nerve to get out of his car. Kiba reacted without any thought. She seemed to be doing that a lot lately when it came to what she called "the evil twins." She flew out the already bent door, ran up to Avith empty-handed having left her .38 in the trailer, got as close to his face as possible, and seethed, *"What are you doing here?"* Avith turned beet red, stuttering and stammering, "I...I...I th-th-thought Avim might be here." *"You know good and well he doesn't live here. Get off my property...now!"*

Kiba wasn't sure where all this was coming from. She didn't even recognize her own voice and certainly didn't feel very courageous. Maybe just time, experience, anger, fear—all of that and so much more—had come together and formed this Kiba? But once again, it worked. Evil fled with his cowardice in tow.

Back in the trailer, Chavera was in tears. "Are you crazy?! He could have killed you!" Kiba explained with the only explanation she had at that point—that it seemed evil and cowardice went hand in hand. She also shared with Chavera that she wasn't sure herself where the courage was coming from but at the same time she knew that what she had done was the right thing no matter how crazy it may have seemed.

Crazy worked. That was the end of any trouble from Avith. Avim, though he had moved on with his life going from woman to woman, and even though he had seemingly done a kind thing in allowing her to live for free and work off her rent, was still spreading rumors about Kiba that she learned to laugh off. She was learning to fight battles in a different way.

CHAPTER 10

ALL THINGS NEW

Kiba continued to work and save with every intention of moving far away. She was hoping Chavera would move with her. The only job Kiba had that was full-time was with the local attorney. She was hoping for a job that would at least meet the income of all three jobs once she moved to her far away dream place. Even a local one that paid more would have sufficed for the time. She had no idea that there was a different plan for her life—all she knew was her own plan.

Eventually, a friend in Abilee heard about a local job with a big company and shared that with Kiba. This friend had some pull in that company so she just knew the job must be for her. She would make more money, continue to work her two part-time jobs, and get to move away faster! She was so excited as this friend set up an interview for her. In the meantime, Kiba's wisdom teeth became impacted. *What?!* But the dentist said it would be fast to remove them, and while she would be sore, she would be able to continue with her interview. But that wasn't to be. Kiba failed to recover, becoming so sick she literally had to crawl out of bed on her hands and knees to the bathroom with incessant vomiting. Chavera even took off time from her job to help. She couldn't make the interview, and her friend was very understanding, rescheduling for the next week.

But the next week came. She was no better. The dentist accused her in a roundabout way of making it much bigger than it really was. Her friend once again rescheduled—this time, for a few days later as the job needed to be filled. Kiba had not improved one iota and still could not make the interview. The job was given to someone else. It was only a day or two after that that Kiba was much better and back at work. Disappointed, not understanding—*why? What just happened?*

Soon after, Kiba got word that there was a major new company moving into Abilee, bigger than the one she had applied at previously. Another chance at another good job. They had a good reputation and paid well. But when she applied, she learned she would have to take a test in the next state over which wasn't really that far, and bring her own typewriter for the test. She was so disappointed as there seemed to be no way for her to find time to drive to the test without taking off work which would affect her already small paycheck, nor did she have a typewriter.

But as "the plan that was not hers" would have it, her boss had to go out-of-town the week of the test. This left her time to quickly leave the office as things would not be busy, take the office typewriter that she was familiar with, take the test, and rush back. All things went as planned. Where they had seemed to be no way, a way had been made.

However, Kiba was overwhelmed with the amount of people that had shown up for the test. She wasn't sure how many jobs there were but didn't see how it could be possible that there were that many that required that particular test. So she was pleasantly surprised when, only a few days later, she received a phone call asking her to come in for an interview. She was nervous about telling her boss what she was doing and how she had acquired the interview, but she also knew that not much was kept secret in most small towns, especially Abilee. But her nervousness was unfounded—he was happy for her. He knew Kiba's story, had even been the one to break the news to her of her momma's death that had crushed her world, and wanted nothing but the best for her. He cheered her on even though he was sorry to lose her. She was a hard worker and enjoyed learning as he taught her some of the ins and outs of legal processes.

Hired! Kiba couldn't believe it! It not only covered what she made in her three jobs but then some! *How could it be that she was the one that was hired—at least one of those hired? There were so many!* She almost felt as if someone was looking out for her. That someone she wasn't aware of was pulling strings with more authority than any man on earth could. *But why?* She knew what she had been taught in church. She knew about Jesus and had even repented and given her life to Him but had seemingly taken it back, trusting herself more than Him. *But really? He would do that? He would do that for her?*

Kiba settled into her new job. It was more than she had dreamed of. She loved to learn. She started out in data entry but was quickly moved into the computer lab with a raise and from there moved into the director's office with another raise. She was sent to classes to learn the word processor—the only one the company had and Kiba was the only one who knew how to operate it. She still had somewhat of a plan in the back of her mind to move far away, but the opportunity that had been presented to her right here was quickly causing her plan to fade away.

Then she was presented with an opportunity to buy a cute, small house in the next state that was just across the state line. A beautiful area that wasn't that far away yet seemed to distance her enough from Abilee. It fit her budget, and she would not have to move again. *Was it possible to actually have a place called home again? A safe place?* Kiba snatched it up. Chavera was happy for her but decided to return home to her parents. There was free room and board there. She was happy Chavera could do that while being reminded that wasn't an option for her. But the excitement over what *was* an option sufficed for her.

Since Kiba was the only word processor at her job, she had opportunity to work with almost all of the departments there. In one of those departments was a young man named Gideon. Gideon was handsome and smart and nice and kind. She had not dated in a while, but Gideon had caught her eye and luckily, or as "plan" would have it, she caught his. She seemed to be working with him a lot lately, and they even saw each other at church. One day, Gideon offered his help if she ever needed him knowing she was single and alone.

Not many days after Gideon's offer to help, Kiba got off her carpool van to retrieve her car for the drive home from her job. But someone had tried to retrieve her car before she got there, ripping out the starter and cutting wires, totally destroying any way to start her car. She had flashbacks of evil wondering if someone was actually trying to steal her car or just harassing her. She looked around for help. The van had already left, and there was no one else in sight. Kiba wasn't that far from her house, so she started walking. She wasn't sure what to do but then remembered

Gideon. He had offered to help and seemed pretty smart. Just maybe?

She called him. He came right over. They both drove to her disabled car, and Gideon began to snip and wrap, all kinds of things she didn't understand, for a temporary fix until Kiba could get the car in to a shop. Chavera once again was certain this was an act of evil meant to harass. But Kiba had no proof, and even if she did, she was certain it would be of no help to her.

But the evil act was turned to good for Kiba. Gideon asked her out for a date. She had to smile. Only a plan bigger than hers could accomplish that. Their first date was Thanksgiving Day. She realized that she had a lot to be thankful for—even in the midst of everything else that was not right. Kiba and Gideon enjoyed Thanksgiving at a friend's house and were quite inseparable over the next several months. It was one of those whirlwind romances that turned into wedding bells by the summer of that next year.

Gideon and Kiba worked hard and excitedly saved money for their upcoming wedding. She was giddy over having her grandpa give her away. At the same time, she was painfully reminded that her momma wouldn't be there, but was grateful to at least have her grandma there. Avim was busy spreading rumors about how hurt he was that Kiba didn't choose him to give her away. She briefly entertained thoughts of disbelief filled with anger but decided quickly to only focus on their important day.

Gideon and Kiba had settled into the home she had purchased, and they were busy making it their own. She was given yet another opportunity to move within the company to a better paying job that was in the same little beautiful town where she had bought her house. A job that she was not qualified for with the salary of someone who *was* qualified. *Really?* Kiba went to the interview only at the insistence of the director. He seemed to have taken a liking to her and went to bat for her in ways that didn't make sense to Kiba. She had met with him, explaining just how unqualified she felt. He just smiled and told her to go anyway, that the job was hers if she wanted it.

So Kiba went. She most certainly wanted the paycheck but felt totally inadequate to meet the needs of the job itself. As she met with the interviewer, a nice young man that obviously knew the job and the requirements, Kiba repeated what she had said to the director. The young man smiled, telling her that she came with high recommendations, and he was certain she would do just fine. She wasn't certain at all but took the job anyway and left there wondering what this was all about.

As it turned out, the other part of the company in the town of Abilee was shutting down. The director knew it and immediately sought to protect her. Kiba teared up. Her gratefulness to him was beyond words. *Why her? Of all the people that would be losing their jobs?* Gideon's job was more stable for quite a period of time as he was part of the shutdown.

Eventually, the shutdown was nearing completion, and Gideon's job was coming to an end. He was offered a job within that same company in a different town over three hundred miles away. While things had seemed to settle down and life was much better, Avim was still spreading rumors but this time included Gideon in his rumors, and he didn't even know him.

Kiba and Gideon agreed that the move felt right. They put their home on the market, packed up their stuff, and headed even farther away from Abilee to new territory. Little did Kiba know that this was all a part of "the plan that wasn't hers.".

CHAPTER 11

A LIFE-SAVING MOVE

As Kiba and Gideon settled into their new home in their new town, it felt different—safe, secure, far away from what had been. They settled into a new church with new friends. Gideon's new job provided enough income that Kiba didn't have to work for the first time in her adult life. She settled in making a home, spending time with her new friends, and spending a lot more time with Friend. Friend was still there, still available, still a source of comfort that she couldn't put into words. He had never left her and had even moved with her every time she moved, changing jobs with her every time she changed jobs.

Of all the changes that had taken place in Kiba's life, Friend was constant—never changing. Kiba talked, probably too much, but Friend faithfully listened. Then Friend would talk. Kiba was always amazed at how wise, loving, kind, and gentle Friend was. When she would hear Friend talk, she found herself not wanting Him to stop. She still had so many questions, but getting to know Friend better helped answer some of those questions and made other questions not seem that important. Then there were those questions that would be answered at the perfect time.

Kiba loved her new town, home, friends—and especially her budding relationship with Friend. Everything went from seeming "not right" to "right". Friend just had a way of changing her perspective on things.

Kiba and Gideon decided it was time to expand their family. She was so excited! Just the word "family" made her heart leap for joy even though she still missed the family that she had started with. It seemed in ways such a long time ago, but in other ways like just yesterday. Kiba quickly became pregnant— the picture-perfect pregnancy—no morning sickness, just a little tiredness. She kept up the house, mowed the yard with a push mower as she enjoyed the exercise, did daily exercises, functioned as usual even with a new precious life growing within her.

She wasn't prepared for what happened next. Kiba had started not feeling well in the last month of her pregnancy but felt that was absolutely normal. She found herself two weeks past her due date, wondering if she would ever give birth. That night, Kiba woke in a panic. Pain was radiating up her right arm, across her back, and down her left arm. *This could not be right!* She had never experienced labor before, but she knew something was wrong. She woke Gideon and explained what she was feeling. Gideon immediately thought heart attack, but Kiba, in her stubbornness, wasn't accepting that. *No way!* Then incessant vomiting that wouldn't stop. Then a fever that kept climbing. Kiba couldn't believe what was happening. She had been in picture-perfect health the whole time.

Gideon finally convinced Kiba to let him take her to the emergency room. She relented. She had wanted the picture-perfect delivery too and didn't consider this a part of her plan. They were ushered right in due to the complications Kiba was experiencing. As it turned out, this new town they had moved into was a college town with a teaching hospital that had a great reputation. And while there were only interns available at that time of night, the intern that was assigned to Kiba had the wisdom to detect a life-and-death issue happening in her body. An issue that was rare—related only to first-time pregnancies. An issue that had presented itself to this same hospital only a week before and had claimed the life of that young mom. An issue that Kiba was told could very well claim her life.

Her only chance was an immediate C-section to relieve the stress from her body, but there were still no guarantees. The kind, gentle doctor that had been her physician through this whole pregnancy was standing by her bed by now, gently instructing her to say goodbye to her family and friends. Kiba's fever had risen to almost 105 degrees by now. Blisters had formed in her mouth and on her lips, and she could barely talk, much less think. But the doctor's verdict got her attention, even in that state. She was surrounded by doctors, specialists, nurses, Gideon—and Friend.

Peace—that was what overcame Kiba in the midst of all the commotion. She managed to tell Gideon goodbye and asked him to tell the rest of her family and friends goodbye for her. Gideon had told her that their friends were all outside her door praying. They weren't allowed to come in, so they stood as close as they could, holding hands and interceding on her behalf. Her little girl would be fine, but Kiba might not get to raise her.

As they hurriedly wheeled Kiba to surgery, she continued to feel a peace that words couldn't describe. No friends or family were allowed to go with her into the operating room, but somehow Friend had managed to slip His way in. Kiba smiled! Her forever Friend whom no one could keep from her side.

Kiba's request of Friend was this: "I would like to live and raise my little girl. But if that is not to be, will You see to it that Gideon's next wife calls You Friend too? And that she would love my little girl like I would have, teaching her about You?" Peace—that peace that passes all understanding.

Kiba was barely conscious yet very aware of what was getting ready to happen. The doctor had explained to her that she would not be able to be put to sleep the conventional way—that the only way they could do it would seem very barbaric yet necessary. They would tie her down, press on her throat until she passed out from lack of air, and then inject a solution into the IV to keep her asleep as they performed the C-section. Barbaric was an understatement. But everything they said was true. She was told she would panic. She did. She was told that would be the last thing she remembered. It was.

Kiba woke up to nurses shaking her and calling her name. She seemed to be able to hear them long before she could open her eyes. She was trembling uncontrollably. They kept piling warm blankets on her, but the trembling would not stop. There was a lot of activity in and out of her room—doctors, specialists, nurses, Gideon—and Friend, calm and sure in the midst of all the chaos.

The chaos continued as Kiba began to bleed internally. This seemed to be a big surprise to the doctors that they weren't prepared for. She relapsed into an almost unconscious state due to the high fever that would not go away. The next time she woke, it was from screams coming from her own throat. She was losing blood at such a fast rate there was no time to warm the next bag. Ice-cold blood was being hand-pumped into Kiba's veins so that it would go faster. The nurse apologized with tears. Finally the bleeding stopped— nine pints later.

Kiba would wake from time to time to see a nurse sitting by her side cross-stitching. The nurse would smile, tell her everything was fine, and check her vitals while she was awake. Friend was also there. Kiba was so glad He didn't need sleep. Gideon was there a lot, taking care of their little girl, bending over to show her to Kiba when she was awake. Her beautiful little girl had a head full of black hair, and her skin was pink and beautiful, like only the skin of a baby born C-section could look—not having been traumatized through a birth canal.

Kiba and Deborah were both in ICU and were quarantined from the rest because of fever. They would bring out Deborah to Gideon on a different schedule than the other babies. So Kiba was elated when a nurse entered her room with Deborah with the intention of Kiba nursing her. *Quarantine over?* She was excited as she sat up in bed. The nurse handed little Deborah off to Gideon who then handed her off to Kiba. She was disappointed that they had wrapped her brand-new little baby girl in a blue blanket. She had wanted things to be as perfect as they could be in spite of the chaotic beginning. Gideon calmly explained that they had probably ran out of pink blankets. Then Kiba noticed her hair had already fallen out. *Wasn't that a little too soon?* Gideon assured her it wasn't. *But Deborah's skin was so perfect yesterday. Why was she so wrinkled and red now?* Gideon explained she must have just had a bath.

So Kiba relaxed and started nursing her little girl for the very first time. Deborah had not nursed more than five minutes when the same nurse that dropped her off came flying into the room with tears. She explained she needed to take Deborah away—because Deborah wasn't Deborah. Deborah was indeed a "boy" who belonged to a new mom who had been deprived of her baby when it was time to nurse because he couldn't be found. Not only that, but the quarantine was *not* over. The nurse was beside herself as she was responsible for not checking armbands. It seemed room numbers had been switched somehow on the charts, and Kiba's first nursing experience was with a baby boy that wasn't even hers. She comforted the nurse as much as she could, extending grace while at the same time challenging her not to let it happen again. The repercussions of such a mistake could span a lifetime.

Kiba settled back in and eventually got to hold and even nurse her little girl. Kiba was grateful for life—for both this precious little girl and her own. She eventually got to go home with little Deborah in tow and Gideon by her side—and Friend, ever faithful Friend.

CHAPTER 12

A LIFE-AND-DEATH LESSON

Two and one-half years later, Kiba and Gideon were anxiously awaiting another little new life. Things couldn't have been better. A healthy, vibrant pregnancy just like the last one. Because of delivery by C-section in her last pregnancy, the doctor recommended the same for this one but was also confident that if Kiba didn't want that, she would be able to deliver normally. Kiba and Gideon prayed. *What would be the right decision?* They felt led to opt for another C-section.

Kiba met with the doctor when the time was near to set a date for the delivery of their precious little boy. As it turned out, the delivery date was only one day after the date of her momma's death. Kiba walked out of the doctor's office with a lot on her mind. She made it home with Deborah in tow, put Deborah down for a nap, sat down on the couch, and declared to herself that she was so glad the date wasn't on the day of her momma's death. She just couldn't handle that.

Enter Friend. Faithful, loving, gentle, kind Friend. And wise. He gently shared with her how God gives life and takes life. He suggested to her that maybe God wanted to change forever how Kiba viewed that awful day. *Maybe she should call the office and ask?*

Kiba knew immediately. *Yes*! Her wise Friend had once again spoken truth wrapped in such peace and gentleness.

Kiba jumped to her feet and ran as fast as an almost full-term pregnant woman can run. Her fingers were shaking as she dialed the phone. The receptionist answered. She asked if the C-section could happen a day earlier. She was told the doctor wasn't on duty that day but that she would ask anyway. Kiba was put on hold. After a few long minutes, she came back to the phone and informed Kiba that she wasn't sure what kind of pull Kiba had, but the doctor immediately said yes to an off-duty Sunday that also happened to be Father's Day. Kiba could barely say thank you through the tears. She hadn't even looked at the calendar yet and did not realize it was Father's Day. Father's Day, ahhh! She had not given much thought to Father's Day from her perspective but had recently started celebrating it as Gideon was now a dad.

Father's Day came, and Kiba found herself in the hospital anxiously awaiting the arrival of little Daniel. What a gift. A son for a dad on Father's Day. The word "Father" was gently rolling off her lips by now with intrigue and wonder.

Kiba's turn came. As it turned out, the C-section had most definitely been the wise decision as little Daniel was a complete breech. Instead of an emergency surgery, a planned surgery. Instead of Daniel's little body possibly being compromised, whole and healthy. Kiba's heart was melting in awe—and it wasn't just the brand-new little life that was melting her heart. It was much bigger, stronger; yet as undeniable as the brand-new life right in front of her.

The day came for Kiba to leave the hospital. Kiba, Gideon, Deborah, Daniel, and Friend—family, leaving together, going home. It was all she had hoped for and even more.

For the next several months, she was busy with a toddler, a baby, friends, church. It had been four years since they had moved to this new town, and it was home.

But then Gideon got a phone call from a friend offering a job right back in the state where Kiba had started out. And she wouldn't be that far from her grandparents. She was torn as everything was so perfect right where they were. Kiba and Gideon prayed. And they knew. They put their house on the market and packed their things. But this time they packed the precious cargo of the gift of two little extra lives. They said a tearful goodbye to fast friends they had made there and set out for home. And of course, faithful Friend went with them.

They arrived back in Kiba's home state and settled in. While she desperately missed her friends they had just left, she quickly made new friends. They found a church home, bought a house, did all the things a normal family does.

Kiba spent a lot of time with Friend and began seeing Him in a different light. While He was most definitely still Friend, she also seemed to be discovering something in Him that surprisingly to her was filling a deep void—a fatherless void. Something that she had never really known from an earthly perspective—what it could be like to have a father. But this surpassed even that.

She knew, even though she had no experience with an earthly father, that Father was filling that void to overflowing, making it okay. Not just okay, but more than okay. Unexplainably okay.

Kiba felt safe, protected, loved, and forgiven. Not that Gideon had not loved and protected her, but a love and protection that no one on earth could provide. A close relationship that just knew—knew no fear—and knew that even though she wasn't aware of His presence at the time of so much turmoil in her life, He most certainly was there.

CHAPTER 13

ENLIGHTENED

Kiba was home. As busy as she was being a wife, mom, friend—trying to keep up with all the daily stuff, Kiba was constantly seeking to make time to sit down with Friend whom she now also saw as Father. In fact, as she would converse with Friend, she found herself calling Him "Father." It was becoming her favorite name to call Him. She had so many questions. And He had all the answers. He seemed to know everything. He was so smart! It seemed that no matter what she asked about—past, present, or future things—He knew! And He wisely answered according to what Kiba needed to know and could process at any given time. Kiba learned that her wise Father would just smile gently at her if any question she asked wasn't the right timing for His answer. And by now, she knew He knew what was best and only wanted His best for her. Sometimes, she didn't like not being answered, but when she saw the love in His eyes for her, it immediately seemed to make it okay.

Kiba learned to trust Him. At times, they would walk together hand in hand. And at other times, she would hold on to His extended right arm like a princess. He always made her feel special. A friend, upon hearing Kiba's testimony, had asked her how she came to be the person she was. What she heard herself say came straight from her heart and was truly how she felt. "I feel as if Father gave His angels charge over Heaven explaining to them He was going to get me, gathered up His royal purple robe, and came to my aid." Kiba knew that in a sense that was exactly what happened through Friend.

There were times she would remember her momma, talk to Father about her and lean on His chest being comforted by His every heartbeat. She had come to know that His heart was for her and not against her. Kiba was also comforted by Father, knowing in her deepest inner being that her momma had not died alone. Both Friend and Father were on the scene as always—even in the valley of the shadow of death, comforting like no other could, not even Kiba.

Kiba would ask Him questions such as, "Why did I ever have to be taken away to Abilee in the first place?"

"Oh, My child, I had a plan for you back before you were even born. I knew where you were at all times. No one could stop Me from carrying out My plan no matter where they moved you. I am able to use all things for good for My children."

"What about Deron when he was hit by that car?"

"My daughter, I was there. I provided a safe place for you to stay while at the same time providing everything Deron and Simona needed—breath, strength, endurance, the hospital, doctors, nurses, and even things you were not aware of."

Kiba recalled that the stretch of road they were on that night was pretty much deserted. But the flat tire and ensuing nightmare happened right in front of a house where some of Father's children lived.

"Father, why did it seem our family was always getting separated, like when Deron had to leave to learn to walk again? Why couldn't there have been a place close by even?"

"Precious one, I was always with you and with each one of you no matter how many miles separated you. Nothing can separate you from My love—not even distance."

Kiba recalled that hard year of separation, but at the same time, Deron got to be with their grandparents; and Simona and Kiba were still together—family together—just different.

"Avim, Father, Avim—what was his purpose in my life? I spent my young years fighting him off in so many different ways."

"My treasured child, the fight was not yours. It was Mine. I gave you courage, locked doors, wisdom, everything you needed when you needed it. And even though you didn't see Me, I stood between you and him that day in the hallway of your home."

Kiba couldn't stop the tears. No, indeed she had not seen Father. She had always wondered what had caused Avim to storm off. It certainly wasn't her stature or ability that intimidated him.

Kiba was also reminded of Father's love even for Avim. She had felt in her heart that she had forgiven Avim and was even praying for him to come to know Friend and Father. Avim had been in a bad accident and was in the hospital when Father gently whispered to her heart to go and help. She did. Avim was still Avim, not acknowledging her presence or her help, refusing to look at her, treating her as if she was invisible. But Kiba knew Love sent her. And she also knew that her forgiveness of him and the past was complete.

Love sat and talked with Kiba, and she had never felt so loved and protected. She knew deep in her heart that she was not fatherless nor ever had been. She didn't have to ask who protected her from Avith, either. She already knew. She already knew in her heart that Avith's sudden departure that terrifying night wasn't attributed to him seeing her .38 revolver. She wasn't sure how Father presented Himself; she was just convinced He did.

Then Kiba remembered how she had sought for love all those years in the wrong way. Her heart was broken beyond belief that she had missed Father's love for her all those times and sought what she was looking for from a mere human being.

"Father, how could You have loved me through all of that? I didn't acknowledge You or Your love. I sought man's love. I drowned myself in parties and alcohol. Nothing seemed to be off limits with me. How could You love me so much after all of that? Why would You love me still? I don't understand. I'm so ashamed. I don't deserve You!"

Kiba couldn't stop crying. Father gently wrapped her in His loving, gracious, and merciful arms and held her.

"That's why I sent Friend, Kiba. I knew every moment of your life before you were even born. I knew you would mess up. I knew you needed Friend. That's why I sent the Answer to all your questions long before you entered this world. When you first met Friend, you only allowed Him to be a part of your life—when it was convenient for you or when you needed Him. But Friend is faithful. He hung in there. When you allowed Friend to *be* your life, your entire life, you also recognized Father."

Kiba felt as if her heart would explode. She was overwhelmed by Friend and Father. What more could she possibly need in life?

"Father, thank You! Thank You for Friend. Thank You for sending Him to me and for me. Without Him, I would *still* be a mess. And I would not know You, Father. I would still be fatherless. "Thank You" seems so weak, Father, but since You know all things, I know You know how grateful my heart is. I love You, Father!"

CHAPTER 14

THE PERFECT PLAN

As Kiba continued to walk and talk with Friend and Father, she grew in her understanding of a lot of things. But even the things she didn't understand were bathed in comfort and peace knowing that Father understood.

So many more questions were answered even as she did the necessary and not-so-necessary things of life. She found herself being so grateful to Father for hearing her momma's prayers and allowing her to die the way she had asked to die. Even though Kiba had long been horrified by all of this, that horror had turned to gratefulness. Ahhh, only Father! Kiba learned that she too could ask Father for even the way she wanted to die and Father would answer according to His perfect plan for her life. And He had also taken that awful day of death and turned it to a day of a celebration of life. Ahhh, Only Father!

Not only had He heard and answered momma's prayers for her impending death, but Kiba suddenly realized that Father was still answering momma's prayers for her after all these years. Father, only faithful Father, could not and would not ever forget what momma had asked of Him, continuing to watch over the children He had given her proving to Kiba that her prayers too for her children and others would long outlive her.

As time went on, Kiba continued to see Friend and Father in so many things of her past. He had allowed sickness to come into her life, preventing the interviews for the job she was certain she needed. Then He had provided the job He had for her—even the opportunity to take the test for that job and with her familiar typewriter in tow. He had given her the job He had planned for her, and it became more than she could have ever imagined with a paycheck that was bigger than her ability to earn on her own.

Father also allowed the destruction of the ignition and wires in her car that day to bring Gideon into her life on a more personal level. Gideon was a part of His plan for her life which He made very plain. Gideon had been offered a job in Abilee months earlier prior to his move there and had turned it down.

He had no desire to live in Abilee. He took another job in a different state which then transferred him to Abilee within a few short months.

She was reminded of the move from Abilee to that beautiful town where Deborah and Daniel were born. Kiba was overwhelmed and shed many tears as she suddenly realized Father's protection for her in that move—a life-saving move—not knowing the pregnancy trouble that awaited her, but Father did. He caused her to be in the right place at the right time—close to a teaching hospital. Not only that, but the teaching hospital had just experienced the week before the same rare pregnancy disorder that Kiba had and knew exactly what to do. Kiba wondered for a brief moment why the young mom that had died was not spared too. But she immediately knew that that is one of those things that only Father knows. He has a plan, and it is always perfect and always for the good of His children even when we don't understand it.

And while in that beautiful town, He even gave her Daniel revealing Himself as the giver and taker of life. Kiba believed that Father used what had happened to her in her first pregnancy to cause the doctor to be willing to give up his day off—on a Sunday, on Father's Day—for the purpose of changing that date forever for Kiba. Those four years in that beautiful town were a part of Father's perfect plan for Kiba.

And it was the knowing that He uses all things to bring about His perfect plan that helped Kiba understand some other questions and to come to grips with unanswered questions, such as Avith's daughter. "Why did she have to suffer the way she did?" "Why does it seem she wasn't protected too?" "Why are there so many in this world who would ask the same questions about their lives?"

Kiba's heart was broken for her—for them. Yet Father comforted her once again reminding her of His perfect plan for every single one of them. And Kiba was reminded that just as she had raced through life at some of her lowest points answering her own questions with her own wisdom, relying on her own self, totally missing Friend and Father even though They were always there, so do many others. Kiba was reminded that He wants them to be able to see what she has seen—that their eyes would be opened to see Friend and Father and that in that sight, they would be comforted and strengthened seeing and knowing beyond themselves—way beyond—eternally beyond. Seeing what Father wants to do with what man has done.

Kiba wanted that for them. She wanted protection for her own family as well as Father had done for her. She wanted them to always see Friend and Father even when the dark things of this world would try to cloud their vision. Kiba found herself talking to Father a lot. A lot of times talking too much and not listening enough. While it always felt good and right to tell Father what was on her heart, it was always life-changing to hear His voice—that quiet, gentle voice that speaks to the heart in a way that only His children can hear.

It was one of those treasured conversations with Father that brought about another life-changing chapter in Kiba's life—not only for Kiba.

CHAPTER 15

DAD?

Kiba woke up that morning to the normal everyday kind of things. She got Deborah and Daniel ready for school, loaded them in the car, dropped them off at the car loop, and then drove home to settle down with a quiet cup of coffee—and Father.

She had talked to Father a lot about others, even mentioning the name of her dad,

Yigol, from time to time. Kiba couldn't bring herself to call him "dad", not even to Father. *Besides, wasn't the title of "dad" an earned title?* She couldn't remember much about him, and there had been no contact that she could ever remember since he went off to prison, except for one very surprising event that she had not handled well at all.

It was two weeks after her momma had died. Kiba was sitting at the beloved piano that she and her momma had spent so much time at—both seriously and playfully. Kiba seemed paralyzed—no feelings, no thoughts, nothing—too overwhelmed with grief. There was a knock on the door that sounded like a bomb going off inside of her nothingness thoughts. She robotically moved toward the door and opened it to find a smiling man who readily introduced himself as her dad. Kiba's immediate thoughts had not been kind. *Drop dead! It should have been you and not her! I don't need you, I need her!* And at the same time, she could almost hear Simona reminding her to *be nice.* Looking back, she was amazed that nothingness thoughts could so quickly be turned to anger.

Kiba had invited Yigol in, but she didn't remember much about the conversation. All she remembered is that she couldn't wait for it to be over so she could return to the safety of nothingness. At some point, it was over. He left. Kiba also remembered getting a letter from him shortly after, but she refused to open it and sent it back. She often wondered what it said.

Then there was the contact that the attorney that she worked for at that time made on her behalf. It seemed, per the attorney, that it was in Kiba's best interest to obtain the right to act on her own behalf as an adult. *You can do that? But why would I need to?* Kiba was nineteen when her momma died, and her attorney explained it was for the purpose of being able to buy things she needed that required an adult signature—car, credit cards, etc. But she would need her dad's permission as he was still her dad and had authority to make decisions on her behalf 'til she was twenty-one. Kiba had bristled at that. "He doesn't have the right to get to make decisions concerning me at all!" Ahhh! But legally, he did. Yigol responded readily with his permission for this to take place.

Kiba was catapulted into a short time of courtroom activity as several witnesses testified before the judge that Kiba was certainly capable of making adult decisions. She felt the judge was watching her reactions to everything, so she had applied her then motto of "sink or swim" and did her best to hold back tears as it was explained to the judge just why she needed this piece of paper that would declare her an adult. He granted her that right, and for the next two years it went with her everywhere she went.

So after all this time and in view of everything that had taken place, Kiba was shocked to hear Father tell her He wanted her to call Yigol. This was certainly not what she had planned for the day. Kiba thought about explaining to Father that she didn't have his phone number. But Father gently intercepted that excuse, reminding her that she had knowledge of where he used to work many years ago, and how that would be a good place to start. Kiba then tried explaining to Father the Privacy Act that had been enacted not too long ago, informing Him that even if she called they wouldn't give her his private information. Father just seemed to smile and wait. How patient He was with her.

But at this point, Kiba just couldn't tell Father no. He had always been right before. He had always seemed to know what He was doing—that perfect plan of His. So she looked up the number for the place he used to work so long ago and called it. The ringing sounded louder than normal in her ears, and her heart was pounding. Finally a sweet-sounding voice answered. Kiba didn't know what to say, so she just quickly blurted out the truth. She told the lady Father had told her to contact her dad whom she hadn't seen or talked to in years, that she didn't have any information on him, and this was the only place that she knew of that might.

The lady kindly put her on hold. In the meantime, Kiba was informing Father how this lady was not going to give her Yigol's private information. In a few long minutes, the kind lady returned to the phone and asked Kiba if she was ready with a pen and piece of paper. She was. She wrote quickly with shaking hands everything the lady told her.

Kiba hung up and stared at the piece of paper lying there on the table. *What now?* She knew the answer to that question already. She picked up the phone and quickly hung it back up. *What if he didn't want to hear from her? After all, she hadn't been very nice to him the few times he tried to make contact. And what would she say anyway?* So many questions that only brought fear. Kiba should have known by now that if Father said do it, it meant He had already made a way and would give her everything she would need when she needed it. Father's perfect love had never brought about fear in her.

So she picked up the phone again and dialed, trembling. A lady answered, and when Kiba asked for Yigol, the lady seemed offended. Yigol had started going by his middle name many years ago which made Kiba a suspicious woman calling for this lady's husband. She quickly explained who she was which changed everything. The lady's voice got excited. She begged Kiba not to hang up and ran to get Yigol.

A gentle, quite voice came from the man Kiba called Yigol. He seemed shocked, subdued, yet Kiba felt he was trying his best to let her know he was so glad she had called.

Over the next few years, Kiba came to realize Yigol was a man of few words. Many times, she interpreted that for a lack of interest in talking with her. Yigol very seldom called her. She mainly called him. And most of the time, she only called at the urging of Father. She didn't like that unloved feeling that she felt when he didn't have much to say coupled with the lack of his phone calls to her. It seemed so much like the unloved feeling of her past. *Why would anyone put themselves back in that position?* But Father kept urging, reminding Kiba of His heart for those who couldn't *see* Him just as had been His heart for her—yes, even for Yigol.

The day came when Father required something new of Kiba. She felt herself putting on the brakes. "*What?!* How could You require that of me, Father?" Even as Kiba was saying that she was ashamed that once again, it seemed she had forgotten Father's perfect plan was perfect. That Father's heart was that all would see Him through faithful Friend, even Yigol.

"But, Father! Yigol doesn't deserve to be called "dad!" Those words rang loud from Kiba's mouth and went straight back into her own ears. Before she even finished hearing herself say that, Father, once again, gently, kindly, yet firmly corrected her. "Kiba, nor have you ever done anything to deserve to be called My child."

Kiba immediately recalled the many messes she had made in life, and Father's tremendous and patient mercy and grace. How He had sent faithful Friend, loving her, protecting her, providing for her—even when she didn't acknowledge Him.

She repented with tears, and the next words out of her mouth were "Yes, Father." Kiba made it a point from that time on to call Yigol "dad" at least once in every conversation. The first time was extremely awkward and hard for her, but her dad gave pause, a long pause even for him when that word came out of her mouth. It continued to be a hard thing to do for quite some time, but Father's words, as always, were true and life-changing.

"Father, this is hard!"

"Kiba, I never called you to easy."

CHAPTER 16

DAD IS HOME!

By this time, Kiba had spent over twenty years calling her dad, encouraging him, telling him about Friend. She would even talk to Father on his behalf while they were on the phone. Dad would always humbly listen but would always fall prey to the lie that his checkered past was way beyond Father's desire or ability to forgive.

She even had another opportunity over the years to see her dad face-to-face as his sister, Kiba's aunt, who also knew Friend and Father was dying of a brain tumor. Her plea in a six-page letter to Kiba was that Kiba would attend her funeral with the hopes that she would have an opportunity to share about Friend with her dad again. She had shared about Friend in a letter to her dad and on the phone and then in person at the funeral, but always with the same results, citing the same lie that he had come to believe.

Then that day came. The day that Kiba received a phone call. But not from her dad—from his wife, telling her that her dad had suffered a major stroke. She was afraid. "Father, after all these years, is he going to die without knowing Friend and You?"

Her dad survived but could not speak, and when he tried, only a noise would come out that sounded like "ah-rah-rah." Kiba called, encouraged, talked to Father on his behalf while he listened, continuing to tell him about Friend. And she would always tell him she loved him. Father had given her His heart for her dad.

Several months later, Kiba felt a strong urge to call her dad. She was busy and really didn't want to stop what she was doing but couldn't quiet that urge. She called. Her dad's wife answered as usual and took the phone to him right away. But this time was different. Her normally quiet and reserved dad, even when all he could say was "ah-rah-rah," seemed to be terrified. His "ah-rah-rah"s were loud, being repeated over and over without seeming to even take a breath in between.

Kiba knew this wasn't normal and cried out to the only One who knew what was happening. "Father, I don't know what to do! Is someone hurting him?" Her dad lived many miles away from her. There was no way she could get to him.

Kiba heard a very familiar voice. That calm, gentle, all-knowing voice that she had grown to be familiar with—the voice of loving Father. "Why don't you tell him about Friend Jesus again?" She didn't waste any time. "Dad, are you ready to give Jesus your heart?" His voice went from sheer terror to unbelievable excitement. It seemed he was saying "Yes, that's it! That's it!" Kiba calmly spoke to her dad once again about the greatest Friend she had ever had—Friend Jesus. She encouraged him to just tell Father he was sorry for the way he had lived his life and that he wanted and needed Friend Jesus to help him. She assured him that Father would hear his heart even though he couldn't speak. After all, He heard and interpreted the frantic "ah-rah-rah's." She reiterated to her dad that no one had lived a perfect life, except Friend Jesus. And that it was by His perfect life that he would be able to come to Father because Father sees the lives of His repentant children through the perfect life of Friend Jesus, Father's Son.

Kiba's dad was crying softly yet with a calm and peace that was not heard at the beginning of the call. The peace was so overwhelming that Kiba thought she might drown in it as it seemed to engulf time and space on both ends of the phone and everything in between. After she finished sharing, she gave her dad time to talk with Father from his heart. Then she talked with Father one last time on his behalf, thanking Him for her dad and what Father had just done through His Son Jesus in her dad's heart. Then Kiba spoke her last words to her dad.

"Dad, I know we didn't have much of a father-daughter relationship here on this earth. But I will see you in heaven, and we will start one then. I love you, Dad."

Two days later, Kiba's dad moved home, his final home, forgiven and safe in the arms of Father because of Friend Jesus. Ahhh! Friend! Father!

Kiba was tearfully grateful and comforted as she was reminded of these scriptures from Father's word and personalized them for Yigol: For God so loved Yigol that He gave His only begotten Son, that if Yigol believes in Him (and he did), Yigol would not perish (and he didn't) but have eternal life (and he does); and also, For by grace Yigol was saved through faith, and that not of himself; it was the gift of God, not of works, lest Yigol should boast. (John 3:16 and Ephesians 2:8–9 respectively)

Home—this word too had taken on new meaning for Kiba. Yes, she was back to her earthly home where she had been snatched from. But she had come to realize that her long journey home was not over yet. That her real home in Heaven with Father and Friend Jesus—where her precious momma and dad had moved to already because of their faith in Friend Jesus—was still awaiting her.

> Let not your heart be troubled; you believe in God, believe also in Me. In My Father's house are many mansions; if it were not so, I would have told you. I go to prepare a place for you. And if I go and prepare a place for you, I will come again and receive you to Myself; that where I am, there you may be also. (John 14:1–3)

LETTER TO DAD

Years earlier

Dear Dad,

As I sit here on a boat in the middle of nowhere, God has once again spoken to my heart about you. He loves you *so much*! I was compelled to write this letter to you and once again share His tremendous love for you as He sent His only Son, Jesus, to die for you.

I know you believe that you have been too bad. But God's Word says that no one is good, except for God. Dad, I'm not good. I too have made many mistakes in my life. I have done nothing to deserve this peace that you keep referring to when I talk with you about Jesus. It is only because I have repented that I received God's grace and mercy that brings that peace—and that grace and mercy is for anyone and everyone who will repent. My greatest desire is that you would know that peace too. And that is God's desire for you as well.

I also need you to know that I have forgiven you. I don't hold the past against you just as God has forgiven me and doesn't hold my past against me. He has been more than enough for me over the years and has taken great care of me even when I was unfaithful to Him. And I ask that you too would forgive me for any hurtful things I have done to you.

He knows where you are, Dad. Just talk to Him. Tell Him you're sorry. I am including some verses from the Bible for you to read and think about. Please know that I call your name out to Father on a regular basis, asking that you would understand His deep love for you and His provision through the blood of Jesus to cover all your sins—past, present, and future. I love you, Dad!

—Kiba

All of us, like sheep, have strayed away. We have left God's paths to follow our own. Yet the LORD laid on him the sins of us all. (Isaiah 53:6, NLT)

For this is how God loved the world: He gave his one and only Son, so that everyone who believes in him will not perish but have eternal life. God sent his

Son into the world not to judge the world, but to save the world through him. (John 3:16–17, NLT)

If you openly declare that Jesus is Lord and believe in your heart that God raised him from the dead, you will be saved. For it is by believing in your heart that you are made right with God, and it is by openly declaring your faith that you are saved. (Romans 10:9–10, NLT)

God saved you by his grace when you believed. And you can't take credit for this; it is a gift from God. Salvation is not a reward for the good things we have done, so none of us can boast about it. (Ephesians 2:8–9, NLT)

My Prayer for You

Father,

Thank You for Friend Jesus! Thank You for sending Him for me and for all who are reading this. Thank You for Your promise that You have a plan for our lives—a plan to prosper us and not to harm us, a plan to give us a hope and a future. Father, I ask in Jesus' name that anyone who is reading this, who may not understand why they had to go through the things in life that You allowed them to go through, that right now at this very moment they would be given eyes of understanding. I ask for them that they would believe that *all* things work together for good to those who love You and are called according to Your purpose.

I ask for them that they would not lean on their own understanding of those events but would trust You and acknowledge You and Your presence in all of these things, even if they felt or feel they couldn't see You at the time. And I ask that they would see that You have made a straight way for them even in the aftermath of that event or even in the very present event they may be walking in this very moment.

Father, I ask they would be strengthened with might through Your Spirit in the deepest part of their innermost being, that Christ would dwell in their hearts through faith; that every single one of them would be rooted and grounded in love, comprehending the width and length and depth and height of the love of Christ for them that surpasses their own knowledge.

Father, in the name of Jesus, by the power of Your Spirit, I pray that each one of them would be filled with all Your fullness—the fullness of our God! Help them not to be anxious about the past, the present, or the future, but help them to give it all to You, kneeling before Your throne, pouring out their hearts to You, and picking up Your promised peace—Your peace that passes all understanding that will guard their hearts and their minds in Christ Jesus! I ask that each one of them would overflow with hope by the power of Your Holy Spirit as You fill them with all joy and peace as they believe You.

Father, so let it be unto them as I have asked of You on their behalf according to Your Word, Your will, and Your promises in the precious and powerful name of Jesus— that Name that is above all names. Amen.

Now to Him who is able to do exceedingly abundantly above all that we ask or think, according to the power that works in us, to Him be glory in the church by Christ Jesus to all generations, forever and ever. Amen. (Ephesians 3:20)

So shall My word be that goes forth from My mouth; it shall not return to Me void, but it shall accomplish what I please, and it shall prosper in the thing for which I sent it. (Isaiah 55:11)

SCRIPTURES AND REFERENCES FOR PRAYER

I pray that you are encouraged and strengthened by the Scriptures that follow that were prayed for you—yes, *you*! God sees you and knows who you are, where you are, and what went on and/or is going on in your life even now.

All Scriptures are taken from the NKJV unless otherwise noted. These are in the order they were prayed for you in the preceding prayer.

"…But there is a friend who sticks closer than a brother." (Proverbs 18:24b)

"For God so loved the world that He gave His only begotten Son, that whoever believes in Him should not perish but have everlasting life." (John 3:16)

"For I know the plans I have for you," declares the Lord, "plans to prosper you and not to harm you, plans to give you hope and a future." (Jeremiah 29:11, NIV)

"That the God of our Lord Jesus Christ, the Father of glory, may give to you the spirit of wisdom and revelation in the knowledge of Him, the eyes of your understanding being enlightened; that you may know what is the hope of His calling, what are the riches of the glory of His inheritance in the saints." (Ephesians 1:17–18)

"And we know that all things work together for good to those who love God, to those who are the called according to His purpose." (Romans 8:28)

"Trust in the LORD with all your heart, And lean not on your own understanding; In all your ways acknowledge Him, And He shall direct your paths." (Proverbs 3:5–6)

"Lead me, O LORD, in Your righteousness because of my enemies; Make Your way straight before my face." (Psalms 5:8)

"Thus says the LORD, who makes a way in the sea and a path through the mighty waters." (Isaiah 43:16)

"That He would grant you, according to the riches of His glory, to be strengthened with might through His Spirit in the inner man, that Christ may dwell in your hearts through faith; that you, being rooted and grounded in love, may be able to comprehend with all the saints what is the width and length and depth and height—to know the love of Christ which passes knowledge; that you may be filled with all the fullness of God." (Ephesians 3:16–19)

"Be anxious for nothing, but in everything by prayer and supplication, with thanksgiving, let your requests be made known to God; and the peace of God, which surpasses all understanding, will guard your hearts and minds through Christ Jesus." (Philippians 4:6–7)

"Now may the God of hope fill you with all joy and peace in believing, that you may abound in hope by the power of the Holy Spirit." (Romans 15:13)

"And whatever you ask in My name, that I will do, that the Father may be glorified in the Son. If you ask anything in My name, I will do it." (John 14:13–14)

"For all the promises of God in Him are Yes, and in Him Amen, to the glory of God through us." (Corinthians 1:20)

A NOTE TO YOU FROM ESTHER GRACE

I have never aspired to be an author. This book was written from a direct call of God. As the testimony in this book of God's grace for my dad on his deathbed was shared on two separate occasions, the feedback from hurting people was overwhelming. As I sat at the feet of Jesus one morning, I heard within my heart the sweet, gentle voice of Holy Spirit say to me "To whom much has been given, much is required." (Luke 12:48) I knew what He meant.

Much testimony had been given to me through all the hard things of life—testimony of God's goodness, power, love, protection, presence, etc. And as the psalmist says many times over in all kinds of ways, "I will tell of all Your marvelous works." (Psalm 9:1)

I was certain for just a fleeting moment that God wanted me to literally *speak* of what He had done for me. Immediately I said, "Yes, Lord, but I need You to give me a platform to speak from." But the platform was not what I thought it would be as He graciously and gently yet powerfully called me to write a book.

My first response was "I'm not an author. I don't even know how to begin." My long-suffering, patient, gentle Father reminded me that He was the greatest author of all times and that He would be the one authoring this book through me. I was encouraged to just step into the Jordan, and He would part it. (Joshua 3) And I did. And He did.

What is God calling you to do with all the testimonies of life that He has given you? We are to tell of His marvelous works! Don't be afraid. God will be with you. He will not leave you nor forsake you. (Joshua 1:5b) The outcome of what God calls us to do is not up to us—it's up to Him. We are only called to obedience "casting down arguments and every high thing that exalts itself against the knowledge of God, bringing every thought into captivity to the obedience of Christ." (2 Corinthians 10:5)

Is He calling you to do something you *know* you can't do? That's the best place to be! Total dependence on God! You know it's *got* to be good if it's something you can't do— and that only God can! He is able to give you everything you need to do it. (2 Corinthians 9:8)

Rest in who He is and who you are in Him. Rest in His ability that He wants to manifest in and through you. Allow Him to use you in these last days to His honor and glory for the sake of His kingdom.

> Now may our Lord Jesus Christ Himself, and our God and Father, who has loved us and given us everlasting consolation and good hope by grace, comfort your hearts and establish you in every good word and work.
> (2 Thessalonians 2:16–17)

ABOUT THE AUTHOR

The author lives in Florida with her husband. She has two grown children, a daughter-in-law, and three grandsons—God's modern-day Shadrach, Meshach, and Abednego.